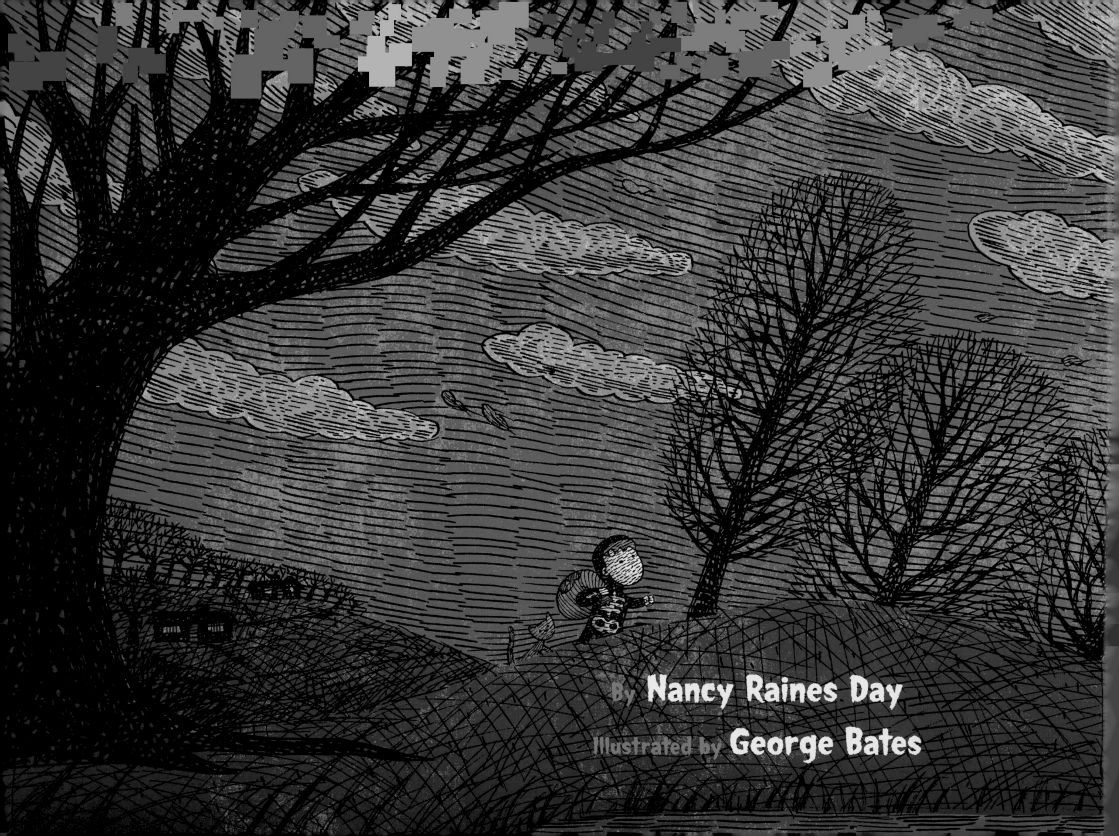

By **Nancy Raines Day**

Illustrated by **George Bates**

On a
windy
night

Abrams Books for Young Readers · New York

On a windy night, on a winding road,
A boy walks home with a heavy load.

On this winding road, on this windy night,
Clouds hide the moon—
and

in

creeps

fright.

Through dark woods and down a hill,

The boy walks fast—and faster still.

What's that? His heart flip-flops with fear.

A whisper rustles in his ear . . .

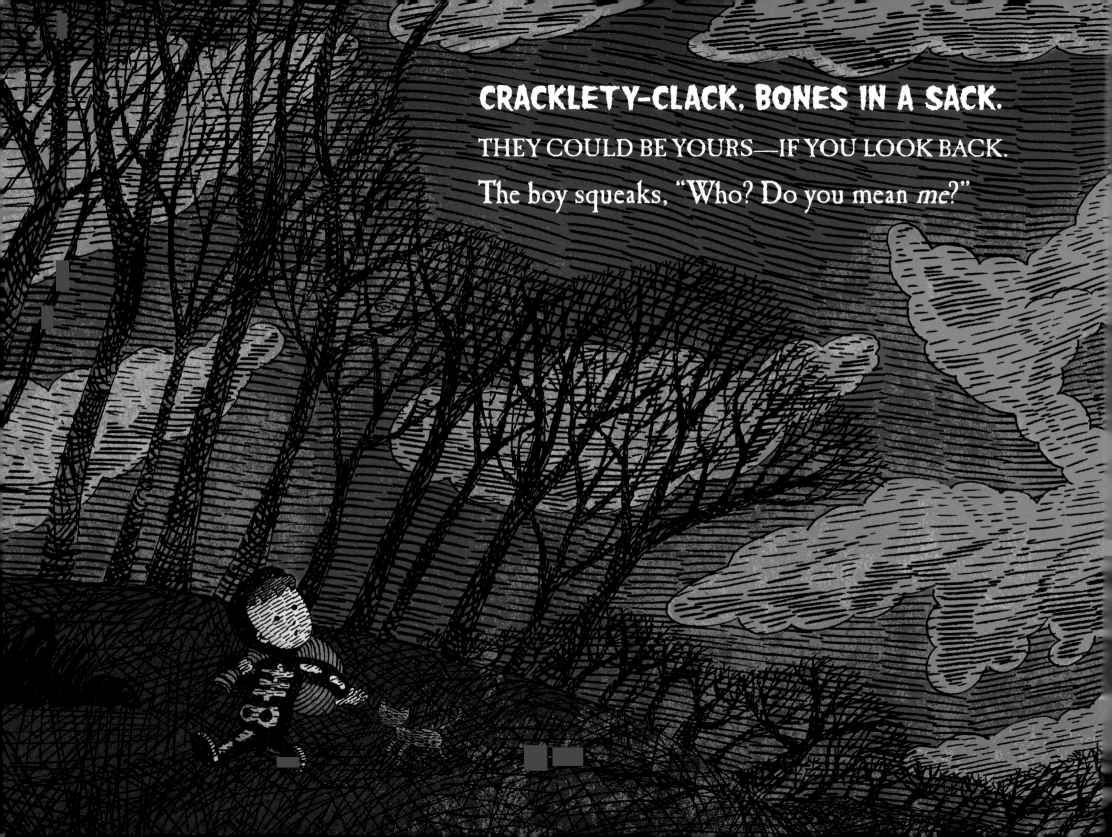

CRACKLETY-CLACK, BONES IN A SACK.

THEY COULD BE YOURS—IF YOU LOOK BACK.

The boy squeaks, "Who? Do you mean *me*?"

"Whooo else?" Owl hoots back from his tree.

The wind blows leaves that brush his face.
The panicked boy begins to race.
But even though he holds his ears,
It's louder now—the voice he hears . . .

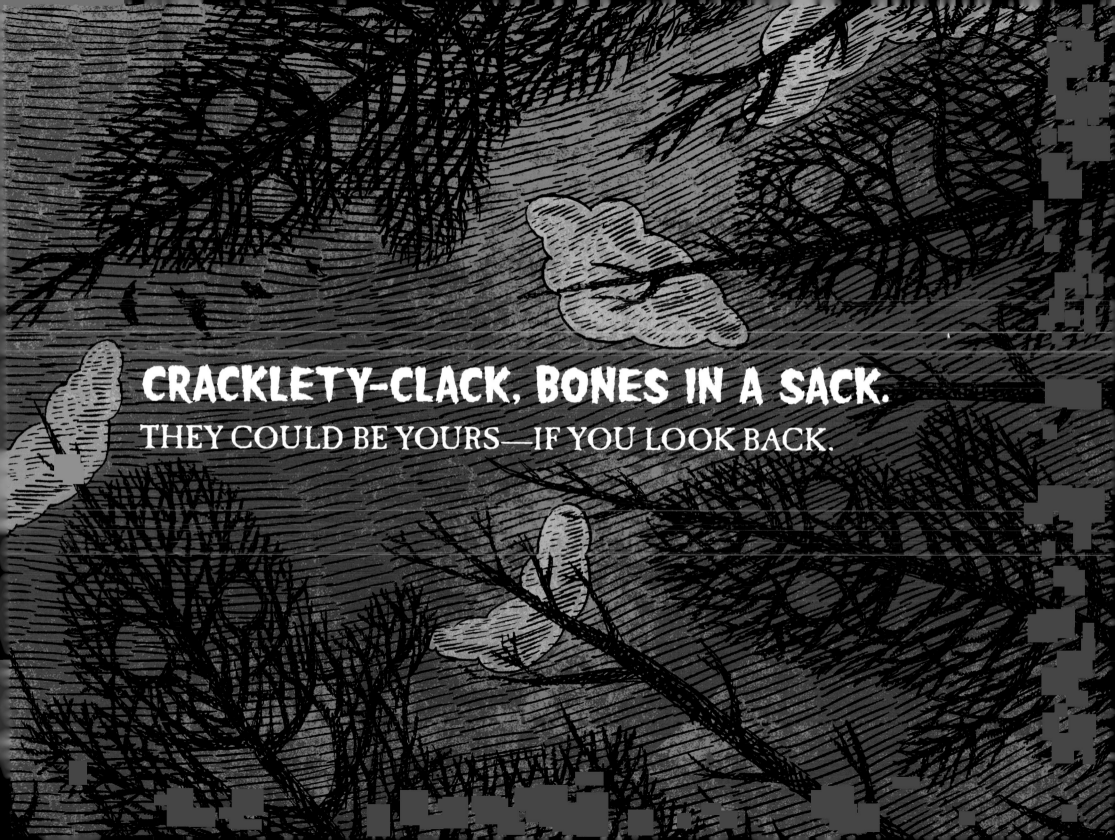

He leaves the spooky woods behind,
But in the field, what does he find?
Real skeletons! They dance in rows,
Clacking knees and crackling toes.

Rough fingers whip his hands and cheek.
He runs, but hears an awful shriek . . .

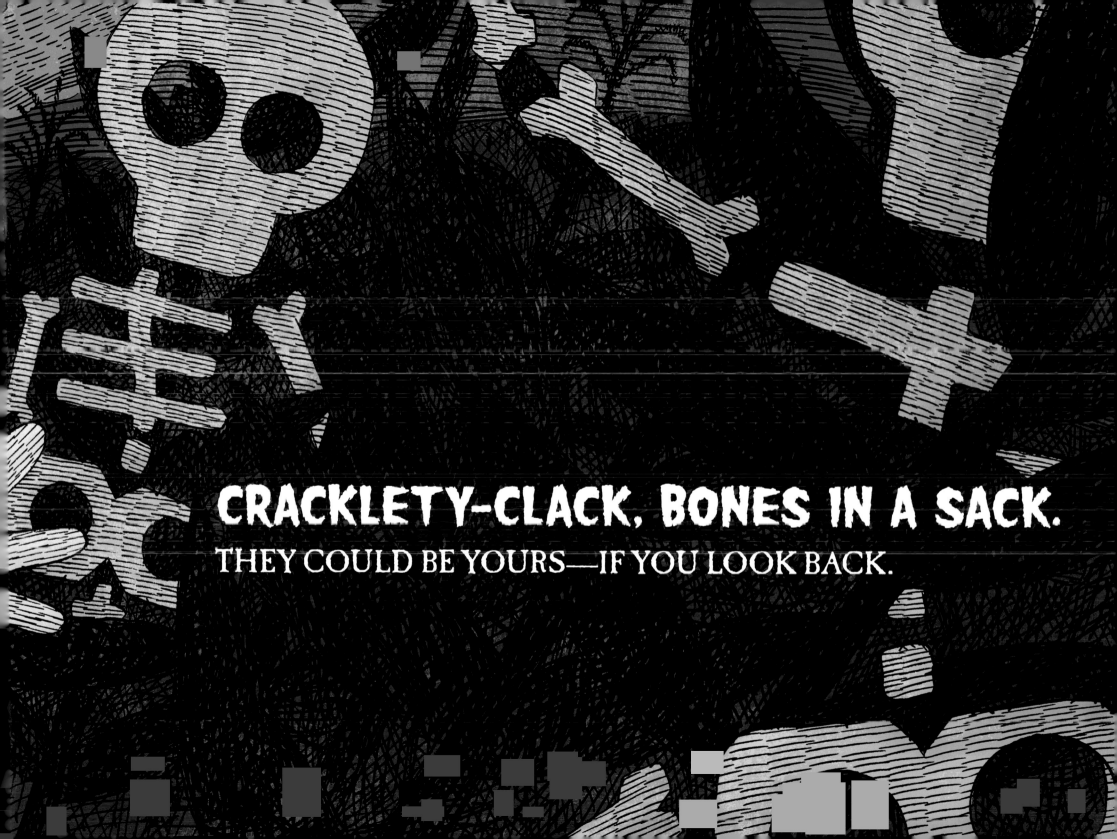

The boy runs blindly. Fast seems slow.
Then—suddenly—he stubs his toe.
He reaches out and feels . . . a head!
It doesn't move. It must be dead.

The boy's feet barely touch the ground.
Again it comes, that deafening sound . . .

He runs so fast. He's breathing hard.
He's almost there. He's in the yard.
A shadow rubs against his legs.
"Don't hurt me, please!" the scared boy begs.

The hairy beast sits on his shoe,
And then it makes a meek . . .

When the clouds roll by, a full moon shines bright.
The boy looks back . . . and laughs outright!

Now dry cornstalks dance where the bones had been.

The head's a pumpkin once again.

So the boy scoops up his purring cat.

They both go home—and that is that . . .

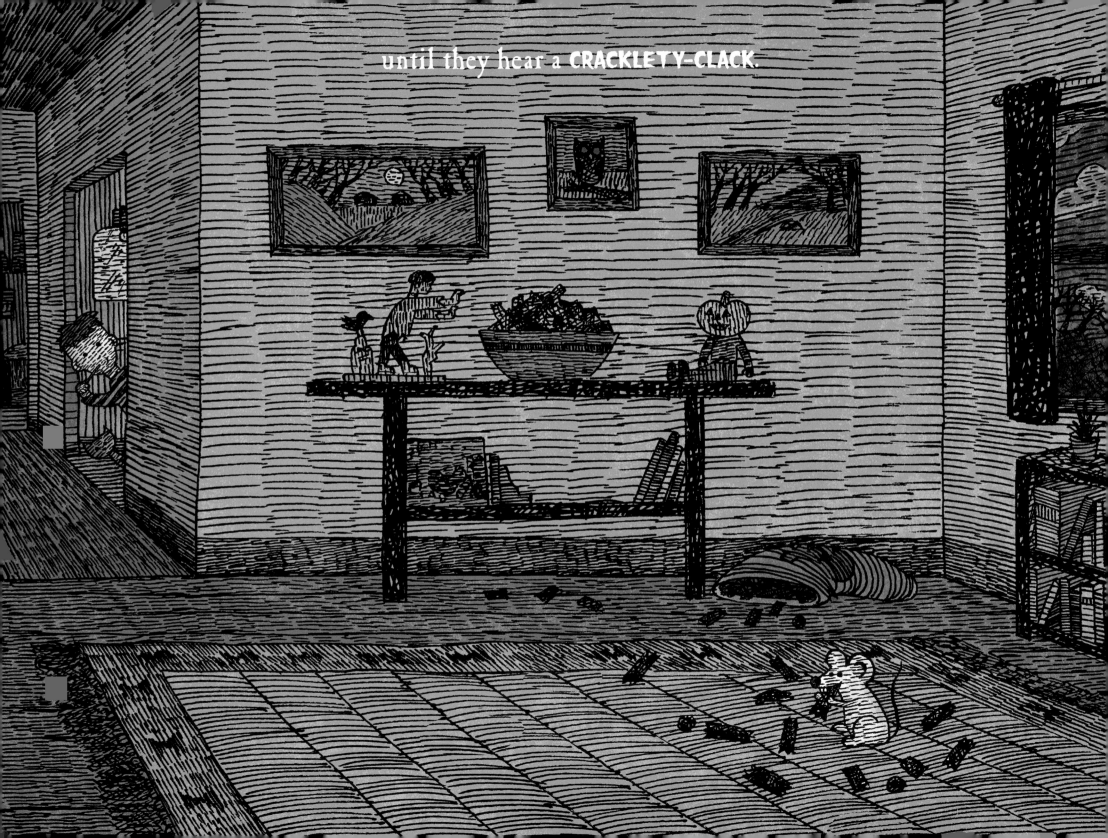

until they hear a **CRACKLETY-CLACK**.

To Shelly, a brave traveler on the winding road. —N. R. D.

For my brother Sean. —G. B.

The art in this book was created with pen and ink on Canson paper, and then scanned
into a computer. The color was added digitally using an experimental techique in Photoshop CS2.

Library of Congress Cataloging-in-Publication Data
Day, Nancy Raines.
On a windy night / by Nancy Raines Day ; illustrated by George Bates.
p. cm.
Summary: On a windy Halloween night, as a boy is returning home through the
woods after trick-or-treating, he hears scary noises behind him.
ISBN 978-0-8109-3900-4
[1. Stories in rhyme. 2. Halloween—Fiction. 3. Fear—Fiction.] I. Bates,
George, 1968 ill. II. Title.
PZ8.3.D3334On 2009
[E]   dc22
2008052532

Book design by Chad W. Beckerman

Printed and bound in China
10 9 8 7 6 5 4 3 2 1

Abrams Books for Young Readers are available at special discounts when purchased in quantity
for premiums and promotions as well as fundraising or educational use. Special editions can also
be created to specification. For details, contact specialmarkets@abramsbooks.com or the address below.

ABRAMS
THE ART OF BOOKS SINCE 1949
115 West 18th Street
New York, NY 10011
www.abramsbooks.com